c D d E e

h l i J j K k

n O o P p

s T t U u

x Y y Z z

Chicka Chicka Boom Boom

Aladdin Paperbacks

New York London Toronto Sydney Singapore

A is out of bed,
and this is what he said,
"Dare double dare,
you can't catch me.
I'll beat you to the top
of the coconut tree."
Chicka chicka
BOOM! BOOM!

by Bill Martin Jr
and
John Archambault

illustrated by
Lois Ehlert

For Arie Alexander Archambault, new baby boom boom-JA
For Libby and Liza, Helen and Morris-LE

First Aladdin Paperbacks Edition August 2000
Text copyright © 1989 by Bill Martin Jr and John Archambault
Illustrations copyright © 1989 by Lois Ehlert

Aladdin Paperbacks
An imprint of Simon & Schuster Children's Publishing Division
1230 Avenue of the Americas
New York, NY 10020

All rights reserved, including the right of reproduction in whole or in part in any form.
Also available in a Simon & Schuster Books for Young Readers hardcover edition.
Printed and bound in the United States of America
10 9 8 7 6 5 4 3 2 1

The Library of Congress has cataloged the hardcover edition as follows:
Martin, Bill.
Chicka chicka boom boom.
Summary: An alphabet rhyme/chant that relates what happens when
the whole alphabet tries to climb a coconut tree.
[1. Alphabet. 2. Stories in rhyme]
I. Archambault, John. II. Ehlert, Lois, ill. III. Title.
PZ8.3.M4113Ch   1989   [E]   89-4315
ISBN 0-671-67949-X (hc.)
ISBN 0-689-84121-3 (pbk.)

Chicka Chicka Boom Boom

A told **B**,
and **B** told **C**,
"I'll meet you at the top
of the coconut tree."

"Whee!" said **D**
to **E F G**,
"I'll beat you to the top
of the coconut tree."

Chicka chicka boom boom!
Will there be enough room?
Here comes **H**
up the coconut tree,

and **I** and **J**
and tag-along **K**,
all on their way
up the coconut tree.

Chicka chicka boom boom!
Will there be enough room?
Look who's coming!
L M N O P!

And **Q R S**!

And **T U V**!

Still more—**W**!
And **X Y Z**!

The whole alphabet
up the–Oh, no!

Chicka chicka...
BOOM! BOOM!

Skit skat skoodle doot.
Flip flop flee.
Everybody running to the coconut tree.
Mamas and papas
and uncles and aunts
hug their little dears,
then dust their pants.

"Help us up,"
cried **A B C**.

Next from the pileup
skinned-knee **D**
and stubbed-toe **E**
and patched-up **F**.
Then comes **G**
all out of breath.

H is tangled up with **I**.
J and **K** are about to cry.
L is knotted like a tie.

M is looped.
N is stooped.
O is twisted alley-oop.
Skit skat skoodle doot.
Flip flop flee.

Look who's coming!
It's black-eyed **P**,
Q R S,
and loose-tooth **T**.

Then **U V W**
wiggle-jiggle free.

Last to come
X Y Z.
And the sun goes down
on the coconut tree...

But—
chicka chicka boom boom!
Look, there's a full moon.